CALENDARBEARS

A Book of Months

To Marilyn Holliday
—*Kathleen and Michael Hague*

Henry Holt and Company, Inc.
Publishers since 1866
115 West 18th Street
New York, New York 10011
Henry Holt is a registered trademark of
Henry Holt and Company, Inc.

Published in Canada by Fitzhenry & Whiteside Ltd.,
195 Allstate Parkway, Markham, Ontario L3R 4T8.

Library of Congress Cataloging-in-Publication Data
Hague, Kathleen.
Calendarbears: a book of months / by Kathleen Hague;
illustrated by Michael Hague.
Summary: Each month of the year a different bear takes part in
an activity that is seasonally appropriate.
[1. Months—Fiction. 2. Bears—Fiction. 3. Stories in rhyme.]
I. Hague, Michael, ill. II. Title
PZ8.3.H1193Cal 1996 [E]—dc20 96-28805

ISBN 0-8050-3818-3

First Edition—1997
Printed in the United States of America on acid-free paper.∞
1 3 5 7 9 10 8 6 4 2
Design: Meredith Baldwin

The artist used pen and ink, watercolor, and colored pencils on
watercolor paper to create the illustrations for this book.

CALENDARBEARS
A Book of Months

By Kathleen Hague
Illustrated by Michael Hague

Henry Holt and Company
NEW YORK

January is new;

winter is old.

Dan bundles up

so his nose won't get cold.

In February Molly writes,
"Will you be mine?"
on the back of
a hand-made valentine.

In March nesting birds

rush to and fro;

Ryan runs after

to see where they go.

With April rains come

new life and spring;

Taylor Ann listens

to glad robins sing.

May buds bloom

a rainbow of flowers;

Catherine works

in her garden for hours.

June days are made
for dreamers like Sue.
Where will she go?
What things will she do?

Stanton loves
the Fourth of July;
fireworks burst
and light up the sky.

Sarah's outside
on a hot August night
watching the fireflies'
magical flight.

September's short days
usher in fall.
The afternoon shadows
make Kevin look tall.

In October Grace calls out,
"Trick or treat."
She's dressed as a pumpkin,
from her head to her feet.

November winds blow;
ripe apples fall.
Drew thinks of the harvest
and gives thanks for it all.

Ellie loves December
and with good reason;
joy is born
in the heart of this season.